HORRID HENRY'S
Rainy Day

HORRiD HENRY'S
Rainy Day

Francesca Simon
Illustrated by Tony Ross

Orion
Children's Books

Horrid Henry's Rainy Day originally appeared in
Horrid Henry and the Abominable Snowman first published in
Great Britain in 2007 by Orion Children's Books
This edition first published in Great Britain in 2012
by Orion Children's Books
a division of the Orion Publishing Group Ltd
Orion House
5 Upper Saint Martin's Lane
London WC2H 9EA
An Hachette UK Company

The Orion Publishing Group's policy is to use papers that
are natural, renewable and recyclable products and made
from wood grown in sustainable forests. The logging and
manufacturing processes are expected to conform to the
environmental regulations of the country of origin.

A catalogue record for this book is available from the British Library.

Printed in China

www.orionbooks.co.uk
www.horridhenry.co.uk

For Joel Simon and Rafael Simon...
you know why

Look out for . . .

Don't Be Horrid, Henry!
Horrid Henry's Birthday Party
Horrid Henry's Holiday
Horrid Henry's Underpants
Horrid Henry Gets Rich Quick
Horrid Henry and the Football Fiend
Horrid Henry's Nits
Horrid Henry and Moody Margaret
Horrid Henry's Thank You Letter
Horrid Henry Reads A Book
Horrid Henry's Car Journey
Moody Margaret's School
Horrid Henry Tricks and Treats
Horrid Henry's Christmas Play

There are many more **Horrid Henry** books
available. For a complete list visit
www.horridhenry.co.uk
or
www.orionbooks.co.uk

Contents

Chapter 1

Horrid Henry was bored.
Horrid Henry was fed up.

He'd been banned from the
computer for rampaging through
Our Town Museum.

He'd been banned from watching
TV just because he was caught
watching a *teeny* tiny bit extra after
he'd been told to switch it off
straight after Mutant Max.

Could he help it if an exciting
new series about a rebel robot
had started right after?

How would he know if it were any
good unless he watched some of it?

It was completely unfair and all
Peter's fault for telling on him, and
Mum and Dad were the meanest,
most horrible parents in the world.
And now he was stuck indoors,
all day long, with absolutely
nothing to do.

The rain splattered down.

The house was grey.

The world was grey.

The universe was grey.

"I'm bored!"
wailed Horrid Henry.

"Read a book,"
said Mum.

"Do your homework,"
said Dad.

"NO!"
said Horrid Henry

"Then tidy your room,"
said Mum.

"Unload the dishwasher,"
said Dad.

"Empty the bins,"
said Mum.

"NO WAY!"

shrieked Horrid Henry.

What was he, a slave?
Better keep out of his parents' way,
or they'd come up with even more
horrible things for him to do.

Chapter 2

Horrid Henry stomped up
to his boring bedroom and
slammed the door.

Uggh.

He hated all his toys.
He hated all his music.
He hated all his games.

UGGGHHHHHH!

What could he do?

Aha.

He could always check
to see what Peter was up to.

Perfect Peter was sitting in his room
arranging stamps in his stamp album.

"Peter is a baby, Peter is a baby,"
jeered Horrid Henry,
sticking his head round the door.

"Don't call me baby,"
said Perfect Peter.

"OK, Duke of Poop," said Henry.

"Don't call me Duke!"
shrieked Peter.

"OK, Poopsicle," said Henry.

"MUUUUM!" wailed Peter.
"Henry called me Poopsicle!"

"Don't be horrid, Henry!"
shouted Mum.
"Stop calling your brother names."

Horrid Henry smiled sweetly
at Peter.
"OK, Peter, 'cause I'm so nice,
I'll let you make a list of ten names
that you don't want to be called,"
said Henry.
"And it will only cost you £1."

£1!

Perfect Peter could not believe
his ears. Peter would pay much more
than that never to be called
Poopsicle again.

"Is this a trick, Henry?" said Peter.

"No," said Henry. "How dare you? I make you a good offer, and you accuse me. Well, just for that . . ."

"Wait," said Peter. "I accept."
He handed Henry a pound coin.

Chapter 3

At last, all those horrid names would be banned. Henry would never call Peter Duke of Poop again.

Peter got out a piece of paper and a pencil. Now, let's see, what to put on the list, thought Peter. Poopsicle, for a start. And I hate being called Baby, and Nappy Face, and Duke of Poop. Peter wrote and wrote and wrote.

"OK, Henry, here's the list," said Peter.

NAMES I DON'T WANT TO BE CALLED

1. Poopsicle
2. Duke of Poop
3. Ugly
4. Nappy face
5. Baby
6. Toad
7. Smelly toad
8. Ugg
9. Worm
10. Wibble pants

Horrid Henry scanned the list.
"Fine, pongy pants," said Henry.
"Sorry, I meant poopy pants.
Or was it smelly nappy?"

"MUUUMM!" wailed Peter.
"Henry's calling me names!"

"Henry!" screamed Mum.
"For the last time, can't you leave
your brother alone?"

Horrid Henry considered.
Could he leave that worm alone?
"Peter is a frog, Peter is a frog,"
chanted Henry.

"MUUUUUUMMMMM!"
screamed Peter.

"That's it, Henry!" shouted Mum.
"No pocket money for a week.
Go to your room and stay there."

"Fine!" shrieked Henry.
"You'll all be sorry when I'm dead."
He stomped down the hall
and slammed his bedroom door
as hard as he could.

Why were his parents so mean and
horrible? He was hardly bothering
Peter at all. Peter *was* a frog.
Henry was only telling the truth.

Boy would they be sorry when
he'd died of boredom stuck up here.
If only we'd let him watch a little
extra TV, Mum would wail.
Would that have been so terrible?

If only we hadn't made him
do chores, Dad would sob.

Why didn't I let Henry call me
names, Peter would howl. After all,
I do have smelly pants.

And now it's too late and we're
sooooooo sorry, they would shriek.

But wait. *Would* they be sorry?

Peter would grab his room.
And all his best toys.

His arch-enemy Stuck-Up Steve could come over and snatch anything he wanted, even his skeleton bank and Goo-Shooter.

Peter could invade the Purple Hand
fort and Henry couldn't stop him.

Moody Margaret could hop over
the wall and nick his flag.

And his biscuits.
And his Dungeon Drink Kit.
Even his … Supersoaker.

NOOOOOO!!!

Chapter 4

Horrid Henry went pale.
He had to stop those rapacious
thieves.

But how?

I could come back and haunt them,
thought Horrid Henry.
Yes! That would teach those
grave-robbers not to mess with me.

**"OOOOOOO, get out of my rooooooooooom,
you horrrrrrrible tooooooooooooad,"**
he would moan at Peter.

"Touch my Goooooooo-shoooooter and you'll be morphed into ectoplasm," he'd groan spookily from under Stuck-Up Steve's bed.

Ha! That would show him.

Or he'd pop out from inside
Moody Margaret's wardrobe.

**"Giiiiive Henrrrrry's toyyyys back,
you mis-er-a-ble sliiiiiimy snake,"**
he would rasp.

That would teach her a thing or two.

Henry smiled.
But fun as it would be to haunt
people, he'd rather stop horrible
enemies snatching his stuff
in the first place.

And then suddenly Horrid Henry
had a brilliant, spectacular idea.

Hadn't Mum told him just the
other day that people wrote wills
to say who they wanted to get
all their stuff when they died?

Henry had been thrilled.
"So when you die I get all
your money!" Henry beamed.

Wow.

The house would be his!
And the car!
And he'd be the boss of the TV,
'cause it would be his, too!!!
And the only shame was . . .

"Couldn't you just give it all
to me now?" asked Henry.

"Henry!" snapped Mum.
"Don't be horrid."

There was no time to lose.
He had to write a will immediately.
Horrid Henry sat down at his desk
and grabbed some paper.

My Will

warning:

do not read unless
I am dead!!!!
I mean it!!!!

If you are reading this
it's because I'm dead
and you aren't.

I wish you were dead
and I wasn't, so I could
have all your stuff.

It's so not fair.

First of all, to anyone
thinking of snatching my
stuff just 'cause I'm dead
 . . . BEWARE!

Anyone who doesn't
do what I say will get
haunted by a bloodless and
boneless ghoul, namely me.
So there.

Now the hard bit,
thought Horrid Henry.
Who should get his things?
Was anyone deserving enough?

Peter, you are a worm.
And a toad.
And an ugly baby nappy
face smelly ugg wibble
pants popsicle.
I leave you . . .

Hmmmm.
That toad really shouldn't
get anything.
But Peter was his brother after all.

I leave you my sweet wrappers.

And a muddy twig.

That was more than Peter deserved. Still…

Steve, you are stuck-up and horrible and the world's worst cousin.

You can have a pair of my socks. You can choose the blue ones with the holes or the falling down orange ones.

Margaret, you nit-face.

I give you the Purple
Hand flag to remember
me by – NOT!

You can have two radishes
and the knight with the
chopped-off head.

And keep your paws off
my Grisly Grub Box!!!

Or else . . .

Miss Battle-Axe, you are
my worst teacher ever.
I leave you a broken
pencil.

Aunt Ruby, you can have the lime green cardigan back that you gave me for Christmas.

Hmmm.
So far he wasn't doing so well giving away any of his good things.

Ralph, you can have my Goo-Shooter, but ONLY if you give me your football and your bike and your computer game Slime Ghouls.

That was more like it.
After all, why should *he* be the only
one writing a will?

Chapter 5

It was certainly a lot more fun
thinking about *getting* stuff from
other people than giving away
his own treasures.

In fact, wouldn't he be better off
helping others by telling them
what he wanted?

Wouldn't it be awful if
Rich Aunt Ruby left him some
of Steve's old clothes in her will
thinking that he would be delighted?

Better write to her at once.

Dear Aunt Ruby

I am leeving you
Something ~~grat REEly~~
~~GREAT~~ REELY
REELy GREAT in
my will, so make sure
you leeve me loads of
Cash in yours.

    Your favorite nephew

        Henry

59

Now, Steve.
Henry was leaving him an old pair
of holey socks. But Steve didn't have
to *know* that, did he.

For all Henry knew,
Steve *loved* holey socks.

Dear Steve

You know your new
blue racing bike
with the silver trim?
Well when your dead
it wont be any use to you,
So please leave it to me
in your will

Your favourite cousin
Henry

P.S By the way,
no need to wait till your dead,
you can give it to me now.

Right, Mum and Dad.

When they were in the old people's
home they'd hardly need a thing.
A rocking chair and a blanket each
would do fine for them.

So, how would Dad's music system
look in his bedroom?

And where could he put
Mum's clock radio?

Henry had always liked the chiming clock on their mantelpiece and the picture of the blackbird. Better go and check to see where he could put them.

Chapter 6

Henry went into Mum and Dad's room and grabbed an armload of stuff.

He staggered to his bedroom and
dumped everything on the floor,
then went back for a second helping.
Stumbling and staggering under his
heavy burden, Horrid Henry swayed
down the hall and crashed into Dad.

"What are you doing?"
said Dad, staring. "That's mine."

"And those are mine," said Mum.

"What is going on?"
shrieked Mum and Dad.

"I was just checking how all this stuff
will look in my room when you're
in the old people's home,"
said Horrid Henry.

"I'm not there yet," said Mum.

"Put everything back," said Dad.

Horrid Henry scowled.
Here he was, just trying to think
ahead, and he gets told off.

"Well, just for that I won't leave you
any of my knights in my will,"
said Henry.

Honestly, some people were
so selfish.

HORRID HENRY BOOKS

Horrid Henry
Horrid Henry and the Secret Club
Horrid Henry Tricks the Tooth Fairy
Horrid Henry's Nits
Horrid Henry Gets Rich Quick
Horrid Henry's Haunted House
Horrid Henry and the Mummy's Curse
Horrid Henry's Revenge
Horrid Henry and the Bogey Babysitter
Horrid Henry's Stinkbomb
Horrid Henry's Underpants
Horrid Henry Meets the Queen
Horrid Henry and the Mega-Mean Time Machine
Horrid Henry and the Football Fiend
Horrid Henry's Christmas Cracker
Horrid Henry and the Abominable Snowman
Horrid Henry Robs the Bank
Horrid Henry Wakes the Dead
Horrid Henry Rocks
Horrid Henry and the Zombie Vampire

Colour Books

Horrid Henry's Big Bad Book
Horrid Henry's Wicked Ways
Horrid Henry's Evil Enemies
Horrid Henry Rules the World
Horrid Henry's House of Horrors
Horrid Henry's Dreadful Deeds
Horrid Henry Shows Who's Boss

Joke Books

Horrid Henry's Joke Book
Horrid Henry's Jolly Joke Book
Horrid Henry's Mighty Joke Book
Horrid Henry's Hilariously Horrid Joke Book
Horrid Henry's Purple Hand Gang Joke Book

Early Readers

Don't be Horrid, Henry
Horrid Henry's Birthday Party
Horrid Henry's Holiday
Horrid Henry's Underpants
Horrid Henry Gets Rich Quick
Horrid Henry and the Football Fiend
Horrid Henry's Nits
Horrid Henry and Moody Margaret
Horrid Henry's Thank You Letter
Horrid Henry's Car Journey
Moody Margaret's School
Horrid Henry Tricks and Treats
Horrid Henry's Christmas Play

Horrid Henry is also available on CD and as a digital download, all read by Miranda Richardson.

HORRID HENRY
Tricks and Treats

Horrid Henry loves Hallowe'en.
He can't wait to go trick or treating.
But surely Mum doesn't expect him to
go out with Peter dressed as a
fluffy pink bunny?

MOODY MARGARET'S School

Why should Horrid Henry spend his precious Saturday playing schools with Moody Margaret? There MUST be a way he can get sent home . . . But how?

HORRiD HENRY'S
Car Journey

Horrid Henry would much rather
be at Ralph's Goo Shooter party
than on his way to a christening.
So watch out, Mum and Dad,
because Henry will do ANYTHING
to stop this journey!

HORRiD HENRY
Reads a Book

A reading competition? No way.
Until Henry hears the prize is a
family ticket to a theme park.
He's determined to win . . .
but how on earth is he going
to read all those books?

HORRID HENRY'S
Thank You Letter

Horrid Henry hates writing
thank you letters. Why should he
thank people for terrible presents?
Then he has a wonderful idea –
one that will make him rich, rich, rich!

HORRiD HENRY and
MOODY MARGARET

Horrid Henry and Moody
Margaret are sworn enemies.
That is, until they find a common
interest – Glop! There's chaos
in the kitchen and Perfect Peter
is in for a surprise.